Adventures of a
LOTTERY
WINNER

Adventures of a LOTTERY WINNER

Hazel Townson

Andersen Press • London

With love to my son Christopher

First published in 2004 by
Andersen Press Limited,
20 Vauxhall Bridge Road, London SW1V 2SA
www.andersenpress.co.uk

British Library Cataloguing in Publication Data available
ISBN 1 84270 332 3

Phototypeset by Intype Libra Ltd
Printed and bound in Great Britain by
Mackays of Chatham Ltd., Chatham, Kent

Cover illustration by Tony Ross

Your library is precious – Use it or lose it!

PART ONE –
JAY'S SECRET DIARY

Wednesday, September 4th

I'm Julie Cairns today. Yesterday I was Jane Crossley but today we're leaving Switzerland, moving from Berne to Manchester so we've all had to change our names again. It's a game we play, Mum, Dad and me. It's fun, but it gets quite complicated. Just before we're about to move I have to learn a whole raft of stuff, like our new address and all our new names and what my dad does for a living, because that always changes too. (Even more important, I have to remember what I mustn't talk about in the new place.) I usually get to keep the same initials for my name, though, to make remembering easier, and I always ask my friends to call me Jay, which covers any possible mistakes.

The Christmas before last, when we left Buenos Aires, Dad bought into this business in Berne, selling classy leather shoes and handbags, all very expensive stuff, but he's got tired of that now. He's pretty restless, my dad. He'll be taking up something different in Manchester before long and I'm hoping it will be fashion this time as Mum and I did well out of the shoes and handbags.

Dad says it's lucky I have a really good memory and can settle in so quickly to every new home, otherwise they might have to board me somewhere. I tell him I don't mind a bit, it's exciting moving around all the time; I never get bored; I've learnt a lot more than any school can teach me, and I've got a cracking collection of souvenirs from all over the world. (Well, that last bit is true, anyway.)

Mum didn't want us to move back to England, which is where we started from when I was a baby, but Dad's sister Blanche lives in Manchester and she's very ill so Dad wants to see her. I think she may be going to die. I guess Mum doesn't like Blanche but I don't know why. You'd think if she liked my dad she'd like his sister as well. Anyway, Mum's already said she won't be going to visit her. She reckons Dad shouldn't go either as it's taking a risk – (maybe Auntie B has something catching?) – but Dad says Mum can please herself; he'll be going there every day. It won't be for long, and Mum can like it or lump it.

A bunch of my Swiss schoolmates came to wave us off when we left for the airport this morning. They all said they didn't want to lose me, and a couple of them even shed a few tears. (Crocodile tears; they won't miss me so much as they'll miss all the treats funded by my rich dad.) I didn't mind about leaving; I'm used to it and I never have enough time to get really fond of anyone. I gave them a big cheery smile and a thumbs-up sign, as I know there will be plenty more hangers-on where I'm going. If you're rich it's never a problem. The problem is finding one person you really like, and who likes you for yourself and not for your money.

I'm writing this in the V.I.P. lounge at the airport. We've been delayed as usual. Dad's having one of his telephone marathons and Mum's drooling over a magazine about famous people's homes. I'm not supposed to keep a diary, but I use an ordinary exercise book and tell them I'm writing a story. Dad's usually suspicious about everything I do, but for some reason he's never got around to checking up on this, and Mum isn't smart enough to work it out. I think I'll be a great novelist one day. I notice things, and I've met so many different kinds of people.

That's us – our gate number just came up, so here we go to yet another new life.

Saturday, 7th September

Well, we made it to Manchester at last, in pouring rain. We're living in this penthouse apartment now, so being on the top floor we should have great views across Manchester and right out to the Pennine hills if the clouds ever lift. We've got a roof garden with trees in great big pots, huge troughs of flowers, and a swing seat under a red and white striped awning. There's even a little fountain out there, and we have a private lift all to ourselves. Dad reckons that's good, because nobody else in the building need ever get more than a quick glimpse of us. He's not very sociable, my dad. My bedroom has a huge walk-in wardrobe, which I intend to fill with new clothes, and at the back of it there's a safe to put valuables in, so that's where my diary goes when I'm not there to keep an eye on it.

As soon as we got here Mum dyed her hair coppery red and started wearing heavier make-up and tinted specs. I nearly didn't recognise her. She calls it her 'English look' but none of the English women I've seen so far look anything like that. As for Dad, he's grown a beard all of a sudden and his eyebrows have thickened up. Maybe there's something in the water!

Despite an argument with Dad, Mum and I have already had two major shopping expeditions – spend, spend, spend! Dad reckons we should do all our shopping on the Internet instead of gallivanting round the town, but Mum insists on browsing properly and trying things on. She told Dad it was the only way to kit me out decently as I'm growing all the time, and anyway it was cruel to keep me cooped up in the flat. Today I got three pairs of designer jeans;

four tops; four sweaters for when the weather turns even worse, which apparently it soon will here; leather boots, jacket and cap; and some luscious silk pyjamas. Between us, we collected so much stuff today that a man from Selfridges's had to help us to carry it all to the car. Mum gave him a really hefty tip so he held the car door and saluted. I think I might grow to like it here.

We've got a maid called Sylvia who works for us six mornings a week. She came with the apartment. She makes the beds, washes up, cleans, takes our dirty laundry away in a shopping trolley and brings it back all ironed and folded next day. I suppose she's a hard enough worker, but she's not very nice looking. Her hands are all red and knobbly, her nose is a bit cockeyed, her roots need doing and she wears far too much blusher. Mum told her she hasn't to go into Dad's study room where he keeps all his papers, because he doesn't want them messed up. I said I didn't want her in my room either, but Mum didn't agree with that. She said somebody had to clear up my mess, and it certainly wasn't going to be her. I didn't think I made much mess, but I know Mum really hates housework. Well, that Sylvia had better mind her own business. None of the foreign maids we've had before ever spoke much English, so I always knew they couldn't read my diary. Let's hope this one just can't read, full stop.

Biggest disappointment is that Dad didn't come up trumps in the fashion industry after all. He's taken up with somebody who runs a van that says BRIAN BRIGHT, PAINTER AND DECORATOR on the side, though Dad's never held a paintbrush in his life. That Brian can't be very bright employing him! Every morning Dad goes off in this van wearing a white boiler suit with paint stains all over it. He even puts paint smears on his face, what you can still see of it! Dad's supposed to be here to see Auntie Blanche, so I can only think he's decorating HER house. Weird! I'm beginning to think England has turned my folks' brains! Let's hope it doesn't do the same to me!

Saturday, September 14th

A whole week of Manchester and I haven't met any new cronies yet. For once in my life I'm getting really bored. I asked Mum if she was going to fix me up with a new school as usual, but she looked a bit shifty and said not this time, we might not be staying long enough. I was horrified as school is my vital point of contact. It's not much fun mooning about in this roof garden on my own and I've been kept on a pretty tight rein since we came to England.

'I've told you; it's different here,' she said.

Sure it is. It's different everywhere we go. So what?

I hardly ever see Dad. He leaves before eight in the morning in that stupid van, and doesn't get home until late, and when he does he's all on edge about something. He's no fun any more. Even shopping with Mum palls after a bit. I really miss school, which is always a doddle for me. I never need to work very hard as I'm usually further ahead than the others to start with. You can't help learning things when you're travelling round all the time.

'Oh, come on, Mum!' I wheedled. 'I really need to go to school, even if it's only for a few weeks. You can't leave me with no one to hang out with.'

She still said no, so I tried sulking for a bit, but it didn't do any good. My mum's as stubborn as a block of concrete.

I was so desperate I actually started to make plans of my own. I thought I might sneak out next Monday and check myself in at the nearest school. Once they know I exist they'll have to give me an education, it's the law. I even found out the names, addresses and telephone numbers of a few local schools. But then something happened to change my mind.

Mum and I were supposed to go shopping first thing, but Mum overslept, so we were still at home when Sylvia turned up for her morning's work. And surprise, surprise! She had somebody with her today – a boy a bit older than me. Sylvia looked flustered when she saw us, as she'd expected us to be out, but she apologised and explained that the boy was her kid brother Clive. She said he usually went to his art class on Saturday mornings, but he couldn't go this week, so she'd brought him along to help. She promised he wouldn't get in the way, but the poor lad looked totally disgusted at the prospect of housework. I should think so, too.

Well, it's an ill wind. He might be miserable, but I suddenly cheered up. Here was a ready-made crony, and a nice change from the snobby lot I usually have to knock around with. He's quite good looking, a lot better than his sister, smoother skinned with light brown floppy hair and big brown broody eyes. I must say he's not much of a dresser, though that might be Sylvia's fault; she's very bossy with him. Still, clothes are something that can easily be put right.

I noticed Mum was looking a bit on edge, as this Clive was already taking in every detail of our lounge, probably deciding what to nick, and I must say we have got some very pricey stuff; it takes ages to pack and costs a fortune to shift every time we move. I reckoned he had that sort of alert and crafty look, like a good shoplifter, so I guessed he might well bring a bit of excitement into my life and fill the gap nicely until I met someone else.

I started off by asking the lad boring questions, such as what was his favourite TV programme and football team and stuff like that, just to get him talking, though the result was mainly mumbles and shrugs. But then Sylvia gave him a duster and told him to start on the table legs. He looked so outraged that I grabbed the duster and gave it back to Sylvia, saying Clive would be much more help in the roof garden. We could do a bit of weeding together.

Mum had already been giving Clive funny looks. Apart from anything else, she obviously didn't fancy a boisterous young lad swishing a duster about near her precious ornaments, so for once she agreed with me.

'Yes, good idea; have a go at the garden,' she said hastily, shooing us towards the door.

Sylvia obviously didn't like to contradict my mum but you could tell she wasn't happy about her brother getting friendly with me. Still, she had to let us go. We didn't do any weeding, of course; I wouldn't have known how, and I'm sure he wouldn't either. We just sat in the swing seat and swapped insults, which gradually turned into proper conversation. Sylvia and my mum both kept poking their heads round the door to make sure we weren't up to any mischief, but they finally gave us the benefit of the doubt and left us to it.

Half an hour later, when my mum collected me to go shopping, I told her Clive was my new friend and I'd like him to come with us.

I'd expected her to argue about that, so I

was ready to pile on the agony, saying I was really lonely and depressed, and if things didn't improve there was no knowing what I might do. I was going to put some pretty strong feeling into that last bit. She scares easily, my mum.

But as it turned out she said she was going to invite him anyway. I was amazed! She was obviously looking for an excuse to get Clive out of the apartment. Sylvia didn't seem so keen. She asked if we were sure it was such a good idea as Clive wasn't much of a shopper.

'He'll soon get fed up,' she told us.

Mum said he'd be fine, I'd keep him entertained. Nobody bothered to ask Clive what he thought, but I guess he was just glad to escape so he came with us anyway, never said a word.

'You two had better behave yourselves,' Mum threatened. 'I've got a busy morning and a late start, and I've had enough messing about for one day.'

I grinned behind her back and winked at Clive, but he didn't return the compliment.

Mum parked the car in a multi-storey and

from there we went straight into the first big store we came to. Naturally Mum made a beeline for the fashion department. She browsed around a bit then decided to try on some dresses. She usually lets me help her choose, but she couldn't very well take Clive in the dressing room with her. So she gave me some money for the coffee bar on the next floor and told us to wait for her there.

Great, I thought, she'll be hours yet and meantime Clive and I can really get to know each other and plan some serious fun.

I told Clive to grab a table while I got the coffees in, but whilst I was in the queue to collect them I turned around and spotted him dodging away. I could hardly believe my eyes. The cheek of him! How dare he treat me like that? After I'd rescued him from the chores as well, the ungrateful so-and-so! I pushed my way out of the queue and flew after him.

I caught him at the top of the escalator and grabbed his arm before he could set off again. I was pretty mad but he told me to keep my cool – it was a free country and he could go off on his own if he wanted to.

'I've got important stuff to do,' he said. 'I'll wait for you on the wall outside your place, so we can go in together when you've finished shopping. If you're there first you wait for me. You'd better not let on to Sylvia that I went off by myself. I'm supposed to be grounded. That's why I got dragged in to yours today.'

'You're not going off by yourself,' I said. 'I'm coming with you.'

'Over my dead body!' he yelled. He gave a sudden twist of his arm, got free and ran off again.

I must admit I panicked, seeing my one chance of friendship disappearing fast. Wherever we've settled people have fallen over themselves to hang out with me. Nobody has ever turned me down in my whole life. So I was blowed if I was going to let this one get away – the first one I'd actually fancied. He ran out of the store so I ran after him, forgetting all about Mum.

That Clive obviously knows all the short cuts around Manchester for we wove in and out of dozens of back streets. It suddenly struck me that if he disappeared altogether I'd have a struggle to find my way back home. Still, I reckoned even getting lost would be worthwhile for finding out what he was up to.

After a bit he turned into a busy road with tramlines down the middle, and came to this great stone building calling itself the City Art Gallery. He went straight up the steps and through the main doors. I'm not a great one for pictures, and I've never been into an art gallery in my life, but I wasn't giving up now.

There was a bloke in uniform standing near the door. He looked me up and down but he didn't say anything or ask for any money, so I just walked in. Clive was well ahead, striding off up this great stone staircase two steps at a time.

When he got to the top of the stairs he disappeared into one of the rooms. By the time I'd made it up there he'd become one of a crowd, all being shepherded about by a bloke who was telling them about the pictures. I dodged in among them before anyone spotted me, and decided to keep an eye on Clive for a bit, to see what he was up to. Maybe he was an art thief, though he seemed a bit young for that.

I soon realised that he'd made himself part of this group on purpose. He seemed to know a lot of them. I counted nineteen kids about his age, most of them boys, plus a smattering of grown-up hangers-on, all clustered round this man who was spouting about the pictures. He could have been a teacher, I suppose. I pricked up my ears, but it was all pretty boring stuff and I soon got tired of listening. So I pushed myself forward, grabbed Clive's arm and pulled him to the back of the group.

'What's going on?' I asked him.

He looked seriously mad. 'Get lost!' he hissed. 'This is my art class, nothing to do with you.'

'You're supposed to be out with me,' I said.

'Wrong! I was supposed to be at this art class until my rotten sister grounded me.'

We were standing in front of this massive picture of a stripy red face with tiny little helicopters dotted all over it, which seemed utterly senseless to me. I told him I couldn't see the point of hanging about in a place like that when there were so many more exciting things to do. He said the pictures were exciting, a lot more exciting than stupid dress shops. So then I said what I thought about the stripy red face.

Clive didn't like that. In fact, he was so mad you'd have thought he'd painted it himself. He called me shallow and said I wasn't really looking at the pictures properly and I was supposed to read the notes to see what they were about. I said pictures shouldn't need notes, there wasn't one picture I liked, and I didn't see what all the fuss was about. He called me ignorant and stubborn, and said I didn't deserve to be rich if I didn't like arty things and was never going to buy them. I told him he hadn't a clue what being rich was like, and he said he didn't want a clue; all rich people were snobs and made their money out of the poor. I said my dad didn't; when he was in Switzerland he made his money out of the rich by selling them real leather shoes with handbags to match, and crocodile briefcases to keep their stocks and shares in.

When I said that, Clive gave me a funny look.

'I didn't know you'd lived in Switzerland,' he said. 'Sylvia thinks you're from the Isle of Wight.'

And I suddenly realised I was talking about our last life when I wasn't supposed to. That's one of the rules of our Changing Game. I always have to be careful not to break the rules, but right then I'd got all worked up and things just slipped out. Too late I remembered that Dad had said something about the Isle of Wight, but for once it had gone in at one ear and out at the other. Well, it's not easy remembering all that new stuff all the time.

'Yeah, well, I just made Switzerland up because you got me mad,' I said, a bit too quickly, 'but my dad could sell shoes and stuff anywhere in the world if he wanted to.

Why not?'

I was going to argue some more, but he turned away and trotted after his group, which had moved on a bit by then. I was mad at myself and a bit alarmed that I'd made such a silly mistake, so I sat down on a bench to recover. In front of me was this great, weird picture of all these little black worms wriggling across the canvas. It really made me shudder and feel itchy all over. I was so busy staring at it in complete bewilderment that I almost missed Clive's lot taking off down the stairs. I had to run to try and catch them up. By then, Clive was chatting away to a girl in the group, a leggy thing with spots all over her chin and hair like a dirty beige doormat. She was wearing a washed-out yellow jumper with a hole in one elbow and some tatty jeans – a real charity case. I heard Clive call her Beth as they shot down the stairs together. I shot after them, all through the gallery and down to the main door, but I got mixed up with another group on the way and somehow I managed to lose Clive's lot altogether. His whole party seemed to have disappeared into thin air. I've thought since that they must have gone into this other building at the back, but I didn't catch on just then.

I wandered around for a while, then gave up. I knew I might not remember how to get home, but I didn't panic. I've been in lots of strange cities, after all, and they've never had to send a search party for me yet. I decided to enjoy the adventure. I followed a sign up to Piccadilly Gardens which I'd noticed on the way in, had a milk-shake and a browse in the shops there, then suddenly came to my senses and remembered my mum. Help! She'd be spitting feathers by this time! I'd better take a taxi back to the store and head for that coffee bar at the double. Hopefully she'd still be trying on frocks. One blessing is, I've always got plenty of money so a taxi was no problem. The trouble was, when I came to tell the taxi driver where to go I found I couldn't remember which store we'd been in, so I headed for home.

Maybe it was just as well I did, because

when I got out of the taxi the first thing I saw was Clive waiting on the low wall outside our apartment block, cool as a Cornetto, ready to go back in with me as he'd planned. I parked myself next to him and said I hoped he was proud of himself, leaving me in the lurch like that. He said he hadn't realised I didn't know my way around, and anyway I'd got home in the end, hadn't I, so what was all the fuss about?

'The fuss is about you ditching me, and my completely wasted morning,' I snapped. 'I thought we were going to be friends.'

'If you don't like art you'll never be a friend of mine,' he said. 'You're as bad as Sylvia. She thinks art's a waste of time, but I'm going to stick with it whether she likes it or not. It's the only thing worth doing and it's all I care about.'

He said that with such passion that he took the wind right out of my sails. He hadn't struck me as the sort that would care so much about anything. (Some novelist I turned out to be!) Well, I certainly didn't want to lose the only chance of friendship

I'd got. So I swallowed my pride and said grudgingly, 'Right then, if it's all so wonderful I suppose I could learn. You'll have to teach me what to look for.'

I could hardly believe I'd just said that!

Anyway, although he looked a bit startled, he didn't rubbish the idea, so I clinched it by asking him to meet me there at ten the next morning. I might have trouble persuading Mum to let me see him again but I reckoned I could manage it if I said art appreciation was part of my education.

'We can go back to the art gallery and have another look,' I said. I'd noticed it was open ten till five on Sundays. 'Maybe if you talk me through it I'll catch on. Just don't bring that scraggy Beth with you.'

That was when Mum burst out of the apartment building like some demented road-rager.

'Where the dickens have you two been?' she demanded, grabbing us by the scruffs of our jackets and scooping us into the lift. She explained that she'd searched the whole store for us, plus the rest of the precinct, and had lost half her shopping time, not to mention her temper. Clive gave me a warning look but I just ignored it and explained that he was studying art and had wanted to show me the art gallery, and what was wrong with that? I insisted that we'd had a very interesting morning and I'd learnt a lot, which made up for not going to school.

While my mum was carrying on, Clive turned laser-beams of hate on me. As for Sylvia, she never said a word, but the minute she saw us she got red in the face and started polishing furiously as if her life depended on it. I guessed Clive would have a pretty thin time of it when she got him home, and serve him right for ditching me! I didn't escape either, for Mum laid into me with all guns blazing the minute those two had gone.

'What did you think you were playing at, running off like that? How many times do I have to remind you that things are different here? You could have been kidnapped for all I knew. Surely you've the sense to realise that people as rich as your dad have enemies? Greedy people who always want what other folks have got. I've done my best to make things easier for you since we got here, taking you shopping and stuff, but you know how important it is to stick to the rules,' she yelled.

Her and her blessed rules!

'You're the one who insists on all that shopping. I can take it or leave it,' I lied, 'and anyway you were glad enough to get rid of us in the coffee bar.' But she ignored that and said I must never wander away like that again or there would be no more treats of any sort. (What does she call treats?) Still, I know she never carries out her threats so I wasn't worried. Dad's the boss, not her. I just waited until she calmed down a bit, then I pointed out that Clive was going to be a real artist, he'd be famous one day and she'd be sorry if she'd stopped me seeing him.

'Clive wouldn't let anything happen to me. He's promised to look after me always,' I lied again.

Mum gave a scornful hoot. 'Have a bit of sense – you hardly know him! And just remember who he is,' she snapped back in her best snobby voice. 'For goodness' sake, why can't you just do as you're told? When Dad hears about this he'll go absolutely berserk! You could have caused a full-blown disaster. Don't you understand?'

Yes, I thought, I'm beginning to understand a lot of things.

Sunday, September 15th

I lay awake for a long time last night, listening for Dad coming home and waiting for the bust-up. Yet funnily enough, although I heard him and Mum arguing away, they left me out of it. Mum seemed to be getting plenty of flak for letting me wander off, and for going out so much herself. I guessed Dad would be saving me for the morning, probably thinking I was asleep. There was much slamming of doors and raising of voices, until well past midnight when I finally did fall asleep.

Sylvia doesn't work on Sundays and I guessed Clive might not turn up either in view of all the fuss. But I was determined to make myself scarce until my folks had calmed down a bit. They aren't early risers on a Sunday, so it wasn't difficult to sneak out before either of them was awake. I was worried that they might hear the lift, so I walked down the stairs and thought I'd never reach the bottom. It's the last time I do that, noise or no noise!

I sat on the wall outside and waited. By half past ten I gave up on Clive and wandered off by myself in the direction of the gallery, guessing that was where he would be.

I was right. When I finally got there, after a couple of wrong turnings, I spotted him huddled in the farthest corner of the gallery snack bar with his scruffy friend Beth.

Beth was just snatching up half a bun that somebody had left on the next table, so they were probably broke, which is why they'd chosen the darkest corner to sit without buying anything.

'Mind if I join you?' I said, breezing along all smiles.

Clive looked embarrassed, and so he should, but he hooked out a chair with his foot and I sat down. I'd made sure I was wearing some of my best gear and could see it was making an impression. Beth was still in her scruffs.

'Who's she?' she asked rudely, so Clive had to introduce us.

'Our Sylvia works for her mum,' he explained.

'Clive and I are quite close friends, as a matter of fact,' I amended. 'Didn't you see me at the gallery yesterday? Clive's teaching me about art.'

Beth burst out laughing. She laughed so much I could see all her back teeth, some of which could have done with decent fillings, not to mention a good brushing.

'I don't see what's so funny,' I said. 'He might well be a proper art teacher one day, if not a real artist.'

'Him?' Beth laughed some more. 'Huh! Pigs might open a butcher's shop!'

Then Clive got mad and rounded on Beth. 'Oh, go on, sneer away! That's what you're good at.' Turning to me, he added: 'She's got some room to talk! She can't draw for toffee. She only tags along to pester me.'

'Don't flatter yourself!' sneered Beth.

'I'm miles better than anybody else in our group and everybody knows it, including you,' added Clive with feeling.

'It makes no difference. You'd still have to go to art college first, and as far as you're concerned college might as well be on the moon.'

'There's nothing to stop him going to art college if he wants to,' I butted in.

That nearly gave Beth hysterics. 'That just shows how much you know. College takes money, birdbrain! Pots of money.'

Ignoring this outburst, I turned to Clive. 'Don't let anybody put you off if that's what you want to do. You can always get a grant.'

'Grant? What planet are you on?' cried Beth. 'Students pay their own fees these days. They borrow from the government then spend the rest of their lives paying it back. That's besides having to eat, of course.'

Suddenly deflated, Clive added gloomily: 'She's right. Can you see Sylvia putting up with that?'

'What about your mum and dad?' I said.

'Sylvia's all the mum and dad he's got,' said Beth.

'Well, there are lots of ways to raise the money,' I pointed out, money never having been a problem for me.

'Oh, sure! Maybe I'll win the lottery when I'm old enough to buy a ticket,' Clive sneered.

That was when I really threw caution to the winds.

'My dad's already won it,' I blurted out.

(Well, he always says he has, whenever I ask him where all our money comes from. He says that's why we have to keep moving around, changing our names and addresses, so he doesn't get begging letters. I guess that's why Mum thinks I'll get kidnapped, too. As if! That just goes to show how neurotic she is.)

They both stared hard at me, then Beth laughed again.

'You're a liar!' she said. 'A barefaced one at that, and I know why. But you can just back off, because Clive's not available.'

'Simmer down; she could be telling the truth,' said Clive. 'What do you know? You've not seen the way they live.'

'Oh, really?' Beth was angry now. 'So she's got everything I haven't! Right then, smarmy Clive, you just go ahead and toady to the rich. Slurp up all the scraps they fancy throwing, why don't you?'

I really hate that girl; she completely ruined the day. I never got my art lesson and in the end I just left them to it. But she'd better watch out; she just might have a few surprises in store.

Monday, September 16th

Well, of course, Dad caught up with me in the end, and this morning I was still smarting from last night's battle. He's pretty fierce when he gets going and the worst of it is I'm grounded now for a whole week at least. I'm forbidden to leave the flat. Just when I've met someone I fancy for once. But that just makes me all the more determined to do what I've been planning all night.

Straight after breakfast Dad went off as usual, and Mum went shopping without me, telling Sylvia to keep an eye on me until she got back.

I decided to make the best of this otherwise wasted time by pestering Sylvia for titbits from the life-story of her family. I must say she wasn't very forthcoming; she was more interested in quizzing me about Brian Bright and the painting and decorating business, though she knew as much as I did about that. She also kept going on about the Isle of Wight, said she might have a holiday there, what was it like and did I recommend it. Yeah, it was great, I said, nice beaches, posh hotels, great sights to see – I've never improvised so much in my life.

Still, I did find out one or two things, the main one being that there really are just the two of them, no parents. One died and one ran off. Sylvia's the breadwinner and can't wait for Clive to leave school and start earning money. She obviously resents being stuck with him and having to bring him up on her own.

'What will Clive do for a living, then? Paint pictures?'

'Oh, he can get that nonsense out of his head right away! He can do a proper job with a proper wage, like other folks have to.'

'Stacking shelves at Tesco's?' I suggested, and she actually agreed.

'Why not?'

This was the moment at which my half-formed plan came full circle. Clive has a dream, a mission in life. His mission needs money. My folks have far more money than they will ever have time to spend. And I know exactly how to get hold of some of it. Two fat bundles, as a matter of fact. And what fun it will be, handing that over in front of bony, bossy, bristly, brainless Beth!

The problem is, just as I was writing this with such glee, Dad turned up unexpectedly and told us Auntie Blanche had just died.

'It was all of a sudden,' he said with a wobble in his voice. 'I mean – I knew it was going to happen, but she seemed all right first thing, then she asked for a drink and by the time I'd fetched it she was gone.'

'Did you get a chance to talk to her?' Mum asked him, which seemed a funny thing to say. He must have been talking to her every day since we got here. Still, he gave a forlorn little nod and flopped onto the sofa. He looked all shaky and he actually had tears in his eyes. It seems he's human after all, and I was really beginning to feel sorry for him – until he started talking about a complete change of plans.

'So that's it,' he sighed. 'There's nothing to keep us here now. We'll need to be on the move again as soon as possible. I've already made a few arrangements.' And sure enough, I spotted the old restless look in his eye.

I can't believe it – we've only just got here and I was starting to feel really at home in England, which is more than I can say for the rest of the world. And what about MY plans? Nobody ever consults me. It looks as though I'm going to lose out as usual. So bang goes my pet scheme for helping a friend in need after all.

Tuesday, September 17th

Dad went out really early, only not in the decorator's van this time. Then Mum took me aside after breakfast and told me the funeral would be on Saturday, but we wouldn't be going to it.

Not going?

I was amazed and said I thought that was the main reason why we came back to England.

'No, your dad just wanted to make his peace with Auntie Blanche, and he's done that. We have to leave Manchester on Friday, and guess where we're going this time? We're flying to Iceland, going to live in the capital, Reykjavik. How about that, eh? Your dad knows somebody who has a fish processing plant up there and can fix him up with a partnership. It's a thriving business, too good to miss, and if he doesn't grab it now he may not get another chance.'

She said Dad had already booked the flights, and my new passport would be ready tomorrow in the name of Jasmine Chadwick. I was to keep it in the safe and not say a word to anybody, least of all Sylvia who doesn't yet know we're leaving.

'Iceland!' I screeched. 'I'm not going off to live in some freezing dump smelling of fish.'

Mum looked shocked.

'Well, I'm not! I'm just not going!' I was getting quite hysterical. 'Of all the rotten, miserable places to pick . . .!'

Mum grabbed my arms and shook them to make me calm down. She said I didn't know anything about Iceland. If I took the trouble to find out what it was like I'd change my mind.

'It's a wonderful country, and I thought

you enjoyed seeing the world? Why do you always have to look on the black side? Why can't you think of it as another big adventure?' And on and on she went.

'Oh, yeah! Frostbite's a big adventure, something I haven't tried yet.'

'Well, you're going, whether you like it or not,' snapped Mum. 'You'll do as your dad says.'

That was when I snapped as well. 'Why should I?' I yelled. 'I've just found a friend I want to stick around with, which is unique for a start, and I'm sick of being carted off from one country to another at the drop of a hat. I never know where I'm going to be from one day to the next. And anyway, he's not my dad, he's just Dave and that's what I'm going to call him from now on.'

This was a secret I'd found out one day back in Sydney, but I'd decided that while life stayed pretty comfortable I wasn't going to declare my knowledge and start a row unless there was a crisis. Well, this was it, a crisis on which Clive's whole future might depend, not to mention mine.

Mum was furious as well as embarrassed, but of course she tried to put me off the scent.

'Don't be ridiculous! I don't know where you've got that silly idea. You're far too clever for your own good, young lady, listening in to private conversations and then getting your facts all wrong!'

After a pause for heavy breathing, she added: 'You've grown very furtive lately. For a start, there's that exercise book you're always scribbling in and trying to hide. Your dad noticed it yesterday. He asked me what it was, and I had to admit I didn't know. So he says he wants to look at it when he gets home tonight.'

Horrors!

Mum must have thought she was being clever, attacking me to get the attention off herself, but it scared me rigid all the same. Dave has a vile temper and I knew that if he found out I was keeping a diary when he'd specially told me not to, I'd probably end up not just in Iceland but in the fish-processing machine as well. So now I don't dare to put my diary back in my little safe. That would be the first place he'd look. I'll have to roll it up, stuff it in the back pocket of my jeans and hide them under my bed. I'll show him one of my old school exercise books instead. It has the same sort of cover and he'll never know.

PART TWO –
JAY'S NOT-SO-SECRET
DIARY

Wednesday, September 18th, mid afternoon

Beth's family – (unemployed dad and elder brother Jack) – lived on the seamy side of central Manchester, in a terraced house that was badly in need of repair. Leaking roof, crumbling plaster, splintered floorboards and cracked windows were the main ingredients of this unsavoury property. Beth, who had never known any other kind of life, was reasonably content to have a bedroom to herself, a place to take her friends, and approachable neighbours who were willing to help out on difficult days when her dad was still in a drunken stupor and there was no money for food. Mrs Kenny next door had a big family and a big heart, and was always ready to exchange a pot of stew or a few helpings of spaghetti and chips for an evening's baby-sitting, so Beth was never likely to starve.

She and her friend Clive had just arrived home from school together this Wednesday afternoon, and were now huddled like conspirators over a dog-eared exercise book which had turned out to be Jay's secret diary.

Beth was wickedly delighted. 'I can't believe it! Did you nick it from her bag?'

Clive explained that Sylvia must have picked it up with Jay's laundry. He had forgotten to ask for any dinner money so he'd gone home for lunch and Sylvia had asked him to stuff the dirty clothes into the washer for her. The diary had just fallen out.

'Did Syl read it herself?'

'She didn't get the chance. I snatched it away and stuffed it in my school bag before she even noticed.'

'I always said it was dangerous to keep a diary,' smirked Beth. 'Just suppose a thing like this fell into the wrong hands. I'd say it would be dynamite, wouldn't you? All that name-changing can't be legal, especially with them getting new passports every five minutes. I wonder where they get them from.'

'I suppose it is a bit dodgy.'

'You bet it is! And it must be true. She wouldn't bother making up stuff like that day after day. What would be the point?'

'You were the one who called her a liar.'

'Well, she does go off the deep end a bit. Have you seen what she says about me, the cheeky madam?'

'Serves you right. You weren't exactly friendly towards her. Anyway, she says she wants to be a novelist. She could just be writing a story.'

'Yeah, her life story. Anyway, you believed that tale about her dad winning the lottery. It looks as though you were right after all.'

Clive took back the diary and tried to smooth it out. He reckoned Beth was getting too wound up. None of this was anything to do with them, true or not, he said. It was private as any diary should be.

Beth didn't agree with that. Of course it was to do with them. It was all about them, wasn't it, so they had a right to read it AND to do something about it.

'I wish I'd never shown it to you now,' grumbled Clive. 'I only did it for a laugh. She'll be frantic that she's lost it, anybody would be. I'll have to sneak it back to her somehow. I daren't give it to nosy Sylvia. I suppose I could post it if I had any money.'

'Post it? You must be joking!' cried Beth. 'Surely you're not stupid enough to miss the point? This girl's taken a shine to you for some reason. She was planning a big handout, TWO FAT WADS! Can't you just picture it? You don't get a chance like that every day of your life. But if you let her leave on Friday you'll miss out after all. She'll just swan off to Iceland and we'll never see her again. Unless we tempt her back with this.'

She grabbed the diary and turned to its back page, on which was scribbled a list of Jay's personal details.

'See these?' She pointed out Jay's home and mobile phone numbers. 'We can ring her up and let her know what's happened. My dad has a phone card we can snitch. Then she'll have to come and see us to get the diary back. And she'll be so grateful she'll bring your nice windfall with her after all.'

Clive frowned. 'That sounds a bit like blackmail.'

He felt somehow responsible for this girl who had written such nice things about him.

'Blackmail? Nothing of the sort!' Beth sounded exasperated. 'Honestly, Clive, you're so thick! We're talking presents here. Didn't you see what she said about the money? She knows how to get hold of some of it. Her folks can easily afford it, and she's dying to give it to you, so who are we to stop her? It's not even as though they earned it with the sweat of their brows so we've nothing to feel guilty about. He's not even her proper dad. Besides, we can't let her go without saying goodbye.'

Clive was looking more and more stubborn, so Beth nagged on. 'You wouldn't turn down a genuine gift, would you, especially from a lottery millionaire? In fact, I reckon it's the duty of folks like that to spread their luck round a bit. Go on, ring her up and ask her to meet us here later today or tomorrow. Tell her the diary got picked up by mistake and you want to hand it back. You won't be asking for anything; she'll be giving. In fact, if she mentions the money you can pretend you don't know anything about it, then she'll think you haven't read the diary.'

'Well, if you're so grasping, why don't YOU ring her? It's your idea.'

'You know what she thinks of me. An invitation will come better from you.'

'It's a waste of time. Sylvia said they'd grounded her so she probably wouldn't get to come out now, even if we asked her. Besides, they'll be busy packing and arranging stuff, and it's bound to be a mad rush if they're leaving on Friday.'

'You're just making excuses because you're chicken!'

'No, I'm not. I'm just being practical. One of us has to be.'

'All right, how's this for practical? We'll go to her. We'll just ask her to come down to street level and we'll wait for her outside the apartment. Surely she can manage that?'

'Maybe so, but who says I want a handout anyway? We're not all money-grabbers. I've still got my pride, whatever you think, and I don't intend to live on charity. Besides, even if she did give me money, Sylvia wouldn't let me keep it.'

'Want to bet? She'd have you down the bank faster than Batman. Anyway, Sylvia doesn't have to know. If you play your cards right . . .'

'Huh! Have you ever tried hiding anything from my sister?'

'You hid the diary, didn't you? Anyway, if you don't want the money, I'll have it. A nice little windfall is just what I could do with.'

'As if she'd give YOU anything!'

They were still arguing when Beth's brother Jack came in with his friend Thomas. The pair of them had bunked off school to roam the city centre in search of pockets to pick but had found themselves being stalked by a possible plain-clothes policeman and had beaten a temporary retreat.

'Anything to eat in here?' demanded Jack, not in the best of tempers.

'Half a stale loaf and two carrots. Take your pick,' said Beth.

'In that case, give us some cash for the chippie.'

Beth said she hadn't any cash.

'You were baby-sitting last night.'

'You know very well I get paid in food. The Kennys are as broke as we are.'

'Do we believe her, Toz?' asked Jack. Thomas shook his head and a scuffle ensued, during which the diary fell to the floor. Thomas abandoned the scuffle to pick it up.

'What's this, then?'

He began riffling the pages of the diary.

'Are you two writing your love story for the *News of the World*?'

'Give that back; it's private.' Clive tried to snatch the diary.

'Nothing's private in this house, kid.' Jack

released his sister and came to see what was happening. 'Give it here, Toz, let's see what you've got.'

Now it was Jack's turn to snatch the diary, at the same time pushing Clive none too gently back against the wall.

Beth was used to her brother's bullying. He and Thomas had both been suspended from school because of it on numerous occasions. Thomas had once hung a Year Seven kid on the school railings by the waistband of his trousers and Jack's most notorious effort had been to lock a lad in the boiler-house for a whole afternoon. Beth knew perfectly well that these two would ruin everything if she didn't act quickly. Jack wasn't exactly literate, but Thomas was, and any minute now those two might find out what was going on.

'It's Clive's notes for his art class, that's all,' declared Beth. 'Nothing there to interest you, but I know what will. If you're really starving there's a couple of packets of crisps on the top shelf in my bedroom.'

'Now you're talking!' Jack dropped the

diary and Beth heaved a sigh of relief.

Back at the apartment, Jay was still recovering from the morning's panic. Who would have thought Sylvia would search under the bed for dirty washing, or strap up the shopping-trolley so securely that nobody else could get into it? At the end of Sylvia's morning shift Jay had been left standing helplessly, watching her wheel that trolley away.

The only way she could think of to get the diary back was via Clive, but he was at school and she was grounded. So now, after a day of incredible anxiety, it was with great relief that she took the phone call from Clive announcing that the diary was on its way back.

'Clive, you're a star!' Her relief was overwhelming. 'I suppose you've read it, but it's just a made-up story so don't get too carried away. Still, I don't want my folks to see it, so when you get here don't ring the bell or anything. Just wait in the street outside the apartment. I'll nip down and collect it.'

This was exactly what Clive wanted. He arranged a time of half past four, but Jay couldn't wait that long. By ten past four she was riding the lift down to street level, desperate to lay hands again on that incriminating document. She ought to tear it up, burn it, bury it, get rid of it somehow.

When she reached the street she saw that it was raining and she hadn't thought to bring a coat. So she sheltered in the wide, imposing doorway, glancing anxiously up and down the street.

Would Clive turn up? He'd let her down before and she wasn't certain she could trust him.

By a quarter to five she was sure he wasn't coming. Then suddenly there he was, riding into view on a battered old bicycle, balancing that scarecrow Beth on the crossbar. Beth was the last person Jay wanted to see, but right now the diary was all that mattered.

Clive gave a wobbly wave and Jay waved back, running out in the rain towards them. Tucked inside Clive's jacket was a damp paper bag that presumably held the diary.

Jay stretched out a hand. 'Thanks ever so much for bringing it back.'

'You're welcome!'

Clive made a move to hand over the parcel, but Beth spun round and snatched the bag from him.

'Hang about!' she said. 'We're doing a swap here. Jay has something for you, Clive. Haven't you, Jasmine, Joy, June or whatever-you-call-yourself?'

'Something for Clive?' Jay's cheeks grew red.

'Well, I CAN read you know, and according to some of these latest entries . . .'

Jay knew very well what Beth was referring to. The trouble was, she couldn't have offered the money now, however much she'd wanted to, as Dave had spirited it away to pay for the new tickets and passports.

'Well, as a matter of fact . . .'

She would have offered some sort of explanation, but she didn't have time to say any more before a shabby dark green van came screeching round the corner and pulled up almost beside her. Two youths leapt out of the van, seized her arms and bundled her into the back. One of them leapt in with her, struggling to hold her still, while the other jumped back into the driving seat and the van sped away. It was all over so quickly that none of them had time to realise what was happening.

Clive was the first to recover, and he was furious.

'Jack and Toz! I might have known.' He turned angrily on Beth. 'So you told them what was going on?'

'I had to; I lied about the crisps and they knew I'd done it to put them off the scent, so they twisted my arms to make me tell. Then they had a confab and decided the girl was worth more than the diary.'

Beth said they hadn't even bothered to try and read the diary. She knew Jack couldn't read more than a few words of it anyway. But once they heard about the lottery that was it.

'It's no use blaming me, though; I never guessed they'd do this. Neither of them are old enough to take a test, never mind drive a van, and how did I know they could get hold of one so quickly?'

'They're easy enough to nick,' said Clive bitterly. 'I expect those two have done it lots of times before. And this is serious now, so you'd better hurry and tell me where they're likely to take her.'

Beth pulled a sulky face. She didn't like the way Clive was rounding on her. Some boyfriend he was turning out to be!

'Where would they take her but our place? They're too thick to think of anything more complicated than that.'

'Right then; your place it is.'

By the time they had cycled back to Beth's house, arguing all the way, Jay was already locked in the attic. The minute they entered the house they could hear her yelling for help at the top of her voice and hammering frantically on the door.

'Told you where she'd be!' cried Beth, charging up the stairs. 'She'll have that door off its hinges if she's not careful!'

'Watch it!' cautioned Clive, thinking Jack and Toz might be in the house.

'It's all right; they'll have gone to dump the van. Quick! This is our chance to grab her before they come back.'

Beth couldn't have cared less about rescuing Jay, but she was anxious to get back into Clive's good books.

'It's all right; I know where they'll have put the key.'

Beth was soon able to unlock the door and Jay tumbled out, shocked, dishevelled and bruised, but not seriously hurt.

Clive caught her and steadied her. Then Jay took one look at Beth and exploded. 'So this is her house, is it? I might have known SHE was mixed up in this!' Turning to Clive, she added, 'I thought better of you, though. I actually thought you were my friend. Silly me!'

Clive felt hurt. 'Well, we HAVE come to rescue you . . .'

' . . . but if you don't want us to bother, we can easily lock you up again,' Beth chipped in, flourishing the attic key.

Clive looked embarrassed. 'Shut up, Beth.'

He started trying to explain about Jack and Toz, but Jay told him to save it, there was no time to waste on talk.

'Just get me out of here. Those two animals will be back any minute. They've only gone to get rid of their crummy van.'

She began running down the stairs and Clive followed, turning his mind to practicalities. One bike was no use for three people.

'Have you any money?' A reasonable question, since Jay had no bag or coat.

'I've always got money. A pocket in every garment, just in case.'

From the back pocket of her jeans Jay produced a fiver, waving it in the air as she ran to the door.

'Right! Then we can all get the bus.'

'I can find my own way home, thanks very much! I reckon you two have done enough damage for one day.'

'That snatch was nothing to do with us, honestly,' protested Clive. 'We got back here as fast as we could on that rickety bike, and we're going to see you safely home whether you like it or not. And that means right up to the door and into the lift.'

'How do I know I can trust you?'

Still, Jay had to admit she felt shaky after her ordeal, and she hadn't a clue which part of Manchester she was in. Besides, she wouldn't fancy her chances if those two kidnappers turned up again.

'All right then,' she decided, 'you can come with me, but not her!'

'I'm sticking with Clive, as always,' threatened Beth. 'Anyway, none of this was my fault either. You don't know what it's like, having a bullying brother like Jack.'

'And you don't know what it's like, being snatched in the street and locked up in a stinky, mucky attic crawling with spiders.'

'For goodness' sake, you two! Belt up and get a move on, unless you want another kidnapping.'

Clive finally managed to shepherd the girls towards the nearest bus stop. Then suddenly, as they rounded a corner they spotted a huge commotion going on ahead of them. It seemed a dark green van had crashed into a garden wall, causing quite a bit of damage.

Loose bricks and shards of glass lay scattered all over the road. A police car had pulled up beside the wreckage and a crowd of onlookers had gathered to enjoy the spectacle.

'Hey, that's it!' yelled Jay. 'That's their van!'

She was right. Jack and Toz were obviously leading characters in this unfolding drama. In fact, it looked as though they were being arrested.

'Serve 'em right!' snapped Jay. 'I hope they get twenty years apiece.'

Seeing what was happening, Clive suggested that Beth had better go and fetch her dad out of the pub.

'If those two are off to the police station to be questioned he'll have to be there.'

Beth groaned, but she knew Clive was right. Similar things had happened all too often before.

'Some fun and games there'll be when Dad sobers up and finds out what's been going on!'

Suddenly the bus arrived and Clive and

Jay leapt onto it, leaving Beth gazing after them, hating Jay, hating Jack and Toz, hating her dad, hating her life.

Clive and Jay sat together in silence on the bus, each thinking over all the details of their short acquaintance. Not much actual time had passed, yet a great deal seemed to have happened. And as a result of all that thinking, by the time Jay finally reached the apartment once more she felt a strange reluctance to go back indoors. Wet, weary and bedraggled as she was, and despite all that had happened, she found that home had lost its welcoming charm. In fact, she didn't really have a home, just a place to sleep until she moved on into a bleak, unsettled future.

She turned to look at Clive. He had escorted her home like a truly chivalrous knight. He had rescued the diary and promised to keep the whole business secret. In fact, he had been a good friend after all, just as she had hoped from the start. She took the diary from him, hesitated for a few seconds then kissed him on the cheek.

''Bye, then – and thanks for everything!'

Clive stood and watched her step into the lift. He stayed there in the pouring rain for a few minutes more, then walked slowly away, like a gambler who has just lost a fortune, not necessarily all in cash.

Wednesday, September 18th, early evening

When Jay walked into the flat she knew immediately that trouble was brewing. Her mother, in floods of tears, came running to meet her, demanding to know where she had been. At first, Jay assumed the tears were for her. Perhaps her mother had witnessed the kidnap and imagined she would never see her daughter again.

But this turned out to be a totally different crisis.

'Your dad's been arrested!' Mum blurted out. 'You'd better sit down. I've got a lot to tell you, a lot of explaining to do.'

Jay had turned very pale, but she said it

was all right, she knew more than her mum might think, and could probably guess the rest.

'I can't say I'm surprised. I've been putting two and two together for quite a while now. Little clues from here and there. I'm not as gullible as you think. Anyway, to crown it all, I came across a shoe-box full of newspaper cuttings when I was looking for my – er – exercise book. Dave's an idiot, leaving that lying about, you know, it was a dangerous thing to do.'

'Almost as if he wanted to be found out. And that wouldn't surprise me, the way he's been acting lately.'

'He didn't win the lottery, did he? He robbed a couple of banks. Ended up pretty notorious. "The Manchester Mole, the most daring bank robber for two decades,"' Jay quoted.

'You know all about it, then? Oh, I'm so ashamed! But I hope you realise I didn't have anything to do with it. Those robberies were all a long time ago, before Dave and I got together. You were just a baby. Your real father had died and I was destitute. Dave was on the run to Australia and he swept me off my feet, not that I had much choice. He took us with him as part of his disguise. In fact, I came to realise later that he couldn't have managed without us. The police weren't looking for a family, just a bloke on his own. But they don't give up searching, all the same, however long it takes, and now they've done it. They've caught up with him at last.'

Mum was in such a state she was actually shaking. Jay sat her down and went to put the kettle on.

'Somebody must have grassed on him, then,' Jay called from the kitchen, 'and I bet it was that nosy Sylvia.'

'No, it wasn't her; it was that low-life Brian Bright with his stupid decorating scam, that's who! He was supposed to be an old friend of Dave's. Some friend!'

Mum was too agitated to sit still. She jumped up, followed her daughter into the kitchen and stood there, twisting her hands together.

'The banks put up a fifty thousand pound reward for any information leading to Dave's arrest, so that greedy snake couldn't resist. I always said I didn't trust him. And I told Dave over and over again that we should never come back to Britain, but he was determined to make his peace with his disapproving sister before she died.'

Jay took a deep breath. She felt thankful Sylvia wasn't involved, as that might have made Clive feel pretty rotten. Even so, despite all her guesswork, this was proving a nasty shock and a great deal to take in, especially on top of a kidnap. Her whole world seemed to be falling apart. Then she thought of something even worse.

'What about you, Mum? Are they going to arrest you as well?'

'I don't think so. Dave's done his best to keep me in the clear. He's not all bad, you know. He made sure he had a very convincing story ready, saying I didn't know anything about his past. He insisted that he tricked me into marrying him, then bullied me into staying when I wanted to leave, and actually it's not all that far from the truth. He said my only crime was being too gullible, and that if I'd ever guessed at the truth I'd have turned him in right away. The police want to interview me again tomorrow, but I don't think they'll do anything drastic.'

That was a relief, at any rate. Another relief was that there would obviously be no trip to Iceland after all. The police had already confiscated all the money and passports. So even in the midst of chaos, Jay could not help a sudden stirring of hope. Maybe she could stay in Manchester after all?

Still, the depressing truth was that if they had no money they couldn't stay in the apartment, so where were they going to live?'

That was when Mum produced the next surprise. Blanche had left a will. Dave had seen it and knew there was nothing for him. But it seemed that Blanche had left her house to Jay, plus quite a bit of money.

'She didn't have any children of her own and she always said she felt sorry for you, having to be dragged round the world like some battered old suitcase. So I suppose that will be available when all this is sorted out.'

Now, that was really stunning news!

'A house of my own? Auntie Blanche's house?' Jay was ecstatic. 'It's a bungalow, isn't it? Dave's talked about it a lot, that big garden with the apple orchard and the little summerhouse. Oh, Mum, that would be perfect!'

'We'll see. There's a lot to get through first. Once this interview is over we'll be able to see which way things are heading. The police will probably want to talk to you as well, so you'd better think carefully about what you're going to say.'

'Oh, that's easy! I'll back up everything Dave's already said. I'll insist that we really believed he'd won the lottery like he said he had. I did believe it for ages.'

'As long as we both stick to the same story,' said Mum. 'We've only ourselves to rely on. Dave won't be able to help us. I'm so used to him making all the decisions, but now we'll have to manage without him.'

Jay thought she could do that quite pain-lessly with no trouble at all.

Then another thought struck her.

'I'll be able to go to school again! To an English school!'

She couldn't keep the thrill from her voice and was already making a mental note to find out which school Clive went to, plus all the details of his extra art classes. Maybe she could take up art herself. Drawing pic-tures couldn't be all that much more difficult than writing novels.

There was suddenly so much to think about, good and bad, that it was a while before Jay remembered to ask the ten thou-sand dollar question – 'What's my REAL name?'

'Your real name?' echoed Mum with a wary look.

'I know I've had so many, but one of them must be real.'

'Well, no, not the travelling ones; we just made them all up. The only real bits were the initials.'

'Yes, but I must have had a birth certificate. Come on, Mum, the police will want to know my real name anyway, and it can't be that bad.'

'All right, it's Jocasta. Jocasta Capano-poulous.'

'You WHAT?' Jay could scarcely believe her ears. 'You've got to be joking!'

'It's Greek. Your father – your real father – was Greek. I met him when I was working in Corfu. Jocasta was his favourite girls' name.'

'Jocasta!' Jay tried it out and it sounded terrible. Then she tried it again and it sounded a little better. Next time, better still. It was certainly different; a name with dis-tinction, on a far higher plane than simple, ordinary Beth. Arty, perhaps; the sort of name Clive might appreciate.

'Oh well, I suppose we'll keep it for great occasions, like weddings and graduations, but I think we'd better add another one as well, for everyday use. And this time I'll pick my own.'

After a pause for thought, she added: 'What about Jacqueline? My friends could

78

call me Jackie. That sounds cool enough. But I draw the line at Capanopoulous – a right tongue-twister! Can't we change that as well? We could do it by deed poll. Or I could take your new name when you divorce Dave and get married again.'

'Stop it, for goodness' sake! How can you keep rambling on, making light of a situation like this?'

'Maybe it's the only way to tackle it. It beats tearing your hair out and foaming at the mouth. Anyway, Mum, you really have got the chance to start a whole new life now, even if it won't be right away.'

Oh, sure! A new life sounded great, thought Mum bitterly. Goodness knew she'd grown sick of the old life, living on her nerves all the time, feeling guilty, waiting for that fateful knock at the door.

Still, she said, 'Do you know, I was a manicurist once. Had my own little salon in Corfu. Do you think I could still make a living at that?'

'Why not?' Jay smiled encouragingly. 'That's the stuff, Mum!'

Jay poured the tea, but the cup and saucer rattled in Mum's unsteady hand.

'You know, Jay,' she mused, 'however clever or careful you are, you can never tell what's waiting for you round the corner, good or bad. Life's nothing more than a lottery when all's said and done.'

A lottery, yes; and there's just a chance I might be one of the winners after all, thought Jacqueline-Jocasta.